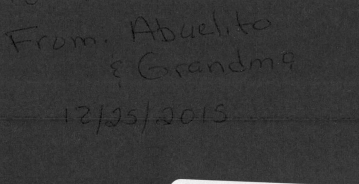

To Alonzo
From: Abuelito
     & Grandma

12/25/2015

ILLUSTRATED CLASSICS

WHITE FANG

JACK LONDON

ADAPTED BY ANNE ROONEY · ILLUSTRATED BY MIKE LOVE

Sandy Creek
NEW YORK

The Northern Wild

The trees loomed, silent and dark, over the frozen water. Nothing moved. It was the deep desolation of the savage Northern Wild.

Then along the frozen river, a string of dogs, their fur bristling with frost, hauled a sled. Two men trudged ahead in silence, saving their breath for walking. On the sled, the clutter of pans, blankets, and an ax was overshadowed by a coffin. It contained a third man—one who had been defeated by the Wild.

As the short day faded, hungry howls rose in the air.

"They're after us, Bill," the man in front said.

Darkness fell, and they made a camp, using the coffin as seat and table.

"How many dogs do we have?" Bill asked.

"Six."

"When I fed them, there were seven. I took six fish and one dog had none. And when I went back, there were six again."

"One of *them*?" Henry said, gesturing into the distance. Bill nodded. The night became a chaos of howls.

They huddled near the fire, a circle of eyes gleaming around them. The dogs whined. At last, the men slept. When Bill woke to build up the fire, he swore there were seven dogs again. But in the morning, there were only five.

"Fatty ran off," he said. "They were onto him so fast I bet he was still yelling as he went down their throats."

After another short day of traveling, they made a camp. Another dog was gone in the morning. The next night, they tied the dogs with sticks near their necks, so they couldn't chew through their leashes. The wolves circled and the dogs whined. One-Ear strained at his leash, pulling toward a wolf that had walked into the light.

"It's a she-wolf," Henry whispered. "She draws the dogs away, and the pack tears 'em apart."

Spanker was gone by morning. That day, the wolves tracked them, the she-wolf falling in behind the sled.

"She's a funny color," Bill said. "Looks more like a husky dog." She fled when he raised a gun.

They camped early. The wolves howled and prowled, bolder than ever, and the dogs yelled in terror.

"I've heard of sharks following ships," Bill said. "Well, them wolves is land-sharks."

"You're half-eaten already if you think that!" said Henry.

They lost no more dogs that night, and started out with new hope the next day. But at midday, the sled overturned. They saw One-Ear bounding over the snow toward the she-wolf. When he saw his mistake, it was too late—the wolves were between him and the sled. He couldn't get back.

Bill took the rifle. They had only three bullets left. He knew that would be no help if the wolves attacked.

"They won't get another of my dogs," he snarled, and set off into the trees.

Henry waited and listened. At last he heard howling and yelps of pain, then three gunshots. Bill did not return.

With only two dogs left, Henry helped pull the sled. He made an early camp, and watched all night as the wolves drew closer to the fire. The next day, he made a wooden platform in a tree and hauled the coffin up to it.

"They got Bill, they might get me, but they won't get you," he said.

That night he threw burning sticks to keep the wolves away. Whenever he dozed, they closed in and his dogs woke him with snarling. The wolves did not move away when morning came.

All day and the next night, he kept the fire burning. He knew it was only a matter of time. He kept a burning stick tied to his hand as he slept. He woke to snarling. The wolves had rushed at him. He fought them with fire, hurling handfuls of burning coals at them. His last dogs were gone already.

At daylight, he built the fire into a circle around him. The wolves sat around the outside of the circle and howled. Next day, gaps appeared in the wall of flame. He sat, drooped over, defeated. The she-wolf stared at him.

"I guess you can come and get me now," he said and fell into an exhausted sleep.

When he woke, the wolves were gone. A team of men, with dogs and a sled, was crashing through the trees. The wolves howled, far in the distance, chasing other prey.

Born of the Wild

It was the she-wolf who first heard the men approaching and was the first to head off. After her came the reluctant pack, led by the lead wolf, a large, gray male. The strongest wolves ran at the front of the pack: the leader, a full-grown young wolf, and an older one with only one eye. The pack moved smoothly, running on through day and night. Though they were gaunt with hunger, their muscles were like steel.

The next day, they brought down a moose, and there was twenty pounds of meat each for forty wolves. The famine over, the pack began to pair off to start families.

At last, the she-wolf was left with the leader, the one-eyed wolf, and the strong, young wolf. Each wanted her as a mate, and they become ferocious. The young wolf lashed out at One-Eye. The older two turned on the young wolf, driving him away. One-Eye approached the she-wolf, and she sniffed him kindly, then led him off into the forest, her choice made.

They ran side by side, hunting, eating, and sleeping together for many days and nights. One night, they came to a clearing, with sounds and smells that drew the she-wolf but that were unfamiliar to One-Eye. It was an Indian village. For two days, they lived by stealing rabbits from the Indians' traps. But the she-wolf was restless. She had grown large and heavy, and was seeking a place that would be quiet and safe.

After two days, she found what she was looking for: a cave hidden in a bank near a frozen stream. The entrance was narrow, but farther back it opened out. She circled around and then curled up inside. One-Eye waited for her, but she made no sign of leaving. He was hungry, so went to hunt. After eight hours, having caught nothing, he returned to the cave. Faint, unfamiliar slobbering sounds from within made him cautious. His mate snarled and drove him away, but not before he had seen the five tiny cubs nestled against her underside. He was surprised, as he had been when this had happened to previous mates. She had never had cubs before, but some instinct made her fear that he was a danger to them so she drove him away.

One-Eye had more luck with his hunting next time. He found a porcupine, but knew to leave it alone. Then he stumbled upon a white bird, a ptarmigan, which he struck down easily with a single paw. He carried it off in his mouth, thinking he would take it back to his hungry family. On his way back to the cave, he saw a lynx stalking the porcupine. The lynx gave up and left after being spiked by the porcupine's spines. The porcupine was curled in a tight ball. One-Eye waited for the porcupine to die. Then he ate the ptarmigan and carried the porcupine back to his mate. She licked his nose and accepted the meat before again driving him away.

The Gray Cub

Only the strongest cub was gray. He noticed that one wall of the cave was different. It was light, not dark like the others, and he was drawn toward it. His mother dragged him back, snarling at him. When he tried to walk through the dark walls he hurt his nose.

The cubs grew, and tumbled around together. But after a time, there was not enough meat. The cubs slept all the time, their life ebbing away. When there was meat again, the gray cub had only one sister left. But it was too late, only the gray cub survived. After the next famine, One-Eye went out and never returned.

The she-wolf left the cub in the cave when she hunted. Slowly, he grew more curious, and one day he discovered that the light wall receded as he approached. He could walk through it! He stood, dazzled by the light, before an unknown world.

At first he snarled in fear. Then he stepped forward and tumbled down the bank. He whimpered and howled, until he stopped rolling. Everything was new and strange—the moss, the rocks, the trees. A squirrel ran away from him, but a moose-bird pecked his nose. He learned as he went along. Living things moved; non-living things stayed still. He found a nest of ptarmigan chicks and ate them all. Their mother appeared and pecked him mercilessly. He ran into a bush and soon saw a hawk swoop down and snatch up the ptarmigan.

When the cub dared to move from the bush, he encountered water. It looked smooth and firm, but he slipped straight through it, his lungs filling with water. Instinct made him swim, and finally the current carried him to the bank. Sleepy, lonely, and feeling helpless he wanted to go home.

As he moved through bushes, he saw a flash of yellow and turned it over with his paw. It was a young weasel. In a moment, its mother leaped out, sinking her teeth into him. He could not shake her off, and it could have been the end of him, but his mother came bounding through the bushes. She flung the weasel in the air, catching it in her jaws. They ate the weasel together.

Every day he grew and learned more of the world, its dangers and its sources of food. Again there was famine, so he hunted through need rather than fun.

The famine broke when his mother brought home a velvety lynx kitten. Full of meat, he slept by her side until woken by snarling. The furious lynx mother was at the cave's entrance. The fight was long and terrible. At one point, the cub sank his teeth into the lynx's leg. It slowed her, and saved his mother a lot of harm. But then he was crushed and had to let go. At last, the lynx lay dead, and his mother badly wounded. For a week they stayed in the cave, eating the lynx and recovering.

Gods of the Wild

The cub hunted alongside his mother, learning the law of meat: eat or be eaten. He thrilled at the chase and at the taste of meat caught live and eaten fresh. He was alive, happy, and proud.

One day, he saw five strange live things crouched by the stream. They did not run away, but sat watching. It was his first encounter with humans. An instinctive sense of awe came over him and he crouched close to the ground. One human stooped to pat him. He snapped at his hand. The man struck the cub's head and the others laughed. Overcome with terror, he cowered, wailing. But then he heard his mother! Soon she was there, snarling.

"Kiche!" called a voice, directed at the she-wolf.

He could not believe what happened next. His all-powerful mother wagged her tail and submitted. His instincts about the creatures' power had been correct.

"There is little dog and much wolf in this one! Kiche was my brother's dog and because my brother's dead, the cub is mine. Look at his white teeth: I will call him White Fang," said Gray Beaver, one of the Indians.

Gray Beaver tied up Kiche. He petted White Fang, which frightened the cub, but felt strangely pleasant.

Soon, the rest of the tribe returned with their dogs. White Fang had never seen dogs, but recognized them as somehow his kind. The pack rushed at him and Kiche, and the Indians beat them away with clubs.

White Fang was awed by the god-like power of the man-animals. Things dead and alive were under their control. They made camp farther than White Fang had ever been, and put up their tents, called tepees.

Exploring the camp, White Fang approached a part-grown puppy, called Lip-lip. It leaped at him, snapping and biting. White Fang fled to Kiche. The same day, he met fire for the first time. Gray Beaver built the fire and White Fang crawled close to explore the leaping orange thing. He burned both his nose and tongue. He leaped back, howling, and the camp laughed at him. He hated their laughter and again crept back to Kiche, who was raging at the end of her leash. White Fang felt overwhelmed and homesick for the silent cave.

Slowly he grew used to camp life. He discovered the men were just, the children cruel, and the women kind. He fought with the other dogs, particularly Lip-lip, who became the bane of his life. White Fang could not play with the other puppies, but was always bullied and beaten by Lip-lip. So he became cunning. One day he lured Lip-lip into chasing him straight to Kiche, who savaged him, ripping his flesh with her fangs.

At last, Gray Beaver untied Kiche. White Fang took her to the forest, to the edge of the Indian camp, but she would go no farther. He felt the pull of the Wild, but she felt the pull of the camp more strongly. He was still too young to go without her.

The Loss of Kiche

Gray Beaver was in debt to Three Eagles, who was leaving camp. To pay his debt, he gave Three Eagles red cloth, a bearskin, bullets—and Kiche. As the canoe pushed off with his mother on board, White Fang leaped into the water and swam frantically after it, ignoring Gray Beaver's shouts. But Gray Beaver set out in his canoe, grabbed White Fang and beat him. Back on land, Lip-lip attacked the hurt and whimpering White Fang, biting at him. But Gray Beaver kicked Lip-lip away—and so White Fang learned that his god-man would protect him. Slowly, he settled into life with Gray Beaver. Although the man showed him no affection, he fed him, and a bond grew between them.

Lip-lip's attacks continued, and White Fang became ever more ferocious and cunning. Always in trouble for stealing food or fighting with the other dogs, he learned to defend himself against the pack, finding that to keep his feet steady on the ground was key to survival. He would rush in, snap, and rush out again. He knew how to knock a dog over and seize him fiercely. He could snarl more ferociously than any other—often that was enough to stop an attack. Soon he was hated by all, man and dog. He was not allowed to run with the pack, so he ran alone. He attacked any other dogs who tried to run with him.

A Chance of Freedom

White Fang still craved the Wild and saw his chance to escape the camp in the fall. As the tribe packed up, preparing to move for winter, he crept away into the forest. Gray Beaver called and searched for him, while he hid, trembling with fear. At last, the camp moved on without him.

The night was cold. The frost bit at his feet. Strange noises in the night frightened him. There was no meat. His time in the camp had softened him, and at the creak of a tree he fled for the village.

It was gone. Standing where Gray Beaver's tepee had once been, he gave out his first long, mournful wolf-howl. For a day and a night he ran, seeking the new camp. He had no food, his muscles were worn, and it started snowing. His coat became bedraggled, and his cut and bruised feet made him limp, but on he went.

By chance, Gray Beaver's tribe had killed a moose and stopped to make camp and eat. When White Fang found their fresh tracks in the snow, he knew he was safe. He followed them to the tepees but then slunk, scared and hurt, more and more slowly toward Gray Beaver's tent. He expected a beating. Gray Beaver raised his hand, and he flinched. But Gray Beaver was breaking off meat—he gave some to White Fang! White Fang, who had chosen to go back to his gods, knew he now depended on them, and would stay.

The Sleds

In December, Gray Beaver set off for Mackenzie, a town down the river. He drove one sled and his son, Mit-sah, drove another. White Fang was to pull Mit-sah's sled, along with seven slightly older puppies. Lip-lip was now Mit-sah's dog, and had been made lead-husky. This made Lip-lip hated by all. Mit-sah gave Lip-lip more meat, encouraging the others to hate him, so that they pulled the sled faster as they chased after him. Although Lip-lip led the sled team, he was no longer in control of the pack. Instead, White Fang led the pack, imposing his rule through strength.

He learned more of the rule of his gods on the months-long sled ride. Once they stopped at a village, and White Fang foraged for scraps of frozen meat where a boy was chopping a moose. The boy chased him with an ax, finally cornering White Fang, who turned on the boy and—against all the rules of his life with the man-animals—bit him. In the outcry that followed, Gray Beaver protected White Fang against the angry Indians. The next day, White Fang came across Mit-sah being bullied by a group of boys—one of them was the boy he had bitten. Snapping and snarling, he drove them away. That night, Gray Beaver gave White Fang lots of meat. Although he did not love Gray Beaver, he was tied to his service and was rewarded and protected in return for protecting his god's property and family.

Famine Again

In spring, they reached the end of the journey. White Fang was a year old. At Midsummer, he met Kiche. His early days came rushing back to him and he bounded toward her joyously. But Kiche snarled and drove him off. She did not remember him, and had new puppies now. She licked and nuzzled them, stopping only to snarl at him. She was a female of his kind, and he would not fight her, so he backed away.

White Fang grew larger, stronger, fiercer, and more solitary. The other dogs learned not to anger him, and Gray Beaver prized him more and more.

When White Fang was three years old, famine came again. The Indians even had to eat their leather slippers, called moccasins. The dogs ate their straps and each other. Some of the Indians died. White Fang crept into the forest and lived on the squirrels and other small animals he could catch. Occasionally he killed a wolf, weakened by hunger. On one of his trips, he met Lip-lip. White Fang was in much better shape, sleek and well fed. He struck out and knocked down Lip-lip easily, then moved in to kill him. It was simple.

At last, he approached the village and heard familiar sounds and smelled cooking fish. The famine was over. He went straight to Gray Beaver's tent, where Gray Beaver's squaw gave him a whole fish to eat. White Fang sat and waited for his god to return.

The Enemy of His Kind

With the loss of Lip-lip, White Fang became leader of the sled team. He hated it. Although he was given extra meat, he had to run in front of the other dogs, which felt too much like running away for him to enjoy. When the dogs were not in harness, they attacked him in a group—they wouldn't dare do it alone. White Fang despised them more than ever.

When White Fang was five years old, Gray Beaver followed the Gold Rush to the Fort at Yukon, hoping to sell furs, gloves, and moccasins to the men on their way to seek gold. They arrived in the summer of 1898, and White Fang saw white men for the first time. He quickly realized they were even more powerful gods than the Indians. They built homes of sturdy logs, and the great steamships that pulled into the bay were their work, too.

But though the men were impressive, their dogs were not. They were of different shapes and sizes, but all were soft and cowardly by the standards of the Wild. White Fang made a game of provoking the dogs that arrived on each steamer so that they would fight him. As soon as he had defeated them, he left. Then the

pack moved in and finished off the dog. So it was the pack, and not White Fang, that met the anger of the white men whose dogs had been destroyed.

Among the men who enjoyed seeing the dogs defeated was one known as Beauty Smith. He was far from beautiful, with a large jaw, a wide face, sloping head, and dirty-yellow eyes and hair. His teeth were yellow, too, and jutted like fangs over his lips. Smith was a coward and prone to rages. He was sometimes unable to contain his excitement when one of the new dogs was about to die fighting. Most of all, he watched White Fang. White Fang hated him instinctively, knowing there was something evil about him.

At first, Beauty Smith tried to persuade Gray Beaver to sell White Fang to him, but Gray Beaver would not part with him for any price. Then Smith, who knew the weaknesses of the Indians, brought whiskey to the camp. Gray Beaver soon acquired a thirst for it and spent the fortune he had earned selling his furs and moccasins on whiskey. Soon he had no money left. Once more Beauty Smith visited.

"You catch'um dog," he said to Gray Beaver, delivering more bottles. When White Fang lay down in the evening Gray Beaver fastened a leather thong around his neck. Soon Beauty Smith came, and Gray Beaver handed him the thong. White Fang snarled and crouched low, and at first would not follow but Beauty Smith hit him with a club. White Fang had no choice but to go with him. But as soon as Beauty Smith was asleep, he bit through the leather and returned to Gray Beaver.

When Beauty Smith came to take him away again, he gave White Fang the harshest beating he had ever had. This time he tied him with a stick to keep his teeth from the leather, but White Fang bit through the stick and returned to Gray Beaver again. Beauty Smith came again, and beat him so hard that he could neither walk nor see. Beauty was a coward, and was cruel as cowards often are. This time he secured White Fang with a chain.

Beauty Smith kept White Fang chained in a cage and tormented him each day. He laughed at him, he goaded him, making him furious and making him hate everything—the chain, the cage, the men who looked at him through the bars, and most of all, Beauty Smith.

One day, Beauty Smith removed the chain and men gathered around the cage. A huge dog, a mastiff, was thrust into the cage. Filled with hate and fury, White Fang leaped at the dog. Though large, it was too slow to defend itself and White Fang attacked it until at last its owner dragged it out. He gave money to Beauty Smith. And so began White Fang's spell as a fighting dog, earning money for Smith from bets. He

came to enjoy the fights. All kinds of dogs were brought, and even once a freshly caught wolf. White Fang defeated them all. He became known as the Fighting Wolf, and his fame spread.

When winter came, Beauty Smith took him up the Yukon to Dawson where men paid 50 cents in gold dust to see him. He was allowed no rest, always prodded and poked and made to fight. It fueled his fury and his hatred. At night, he was taken into the forest for fights. He always won, killing the other dog. Once, he was set against a lynx and had to fight for his life. But after that, nothing was a match for him until the first bulldog came to the area. As soon as it arrived, it was clear that it would have to fight White Fang.

White Fang had never seen such a dog before. Stocky, with a stub of wagging tail, he stood solidly and stared at White Fang.

"Get him, Cherokee!" the crowd urged. The dog's owner, Tim Keenan, stroked him and pushed him forward. White Fang leaped. He was in and out in a flash leaving Cherokee's neck and ear ripped and bleeding. Cherokee made no sound but followed White Fang around the cage. This went on and on, while the dog bled. Both were puzzled by the other's methods. At last, White Fang barged into Cherokee with his shoulder, expecting to knock him over, but the bulldog was too solid and instead White Fang fell over. In an instant, Cherokee sank his teeth into White Fang's throat. Then Cherokee hung on while White Fang whirled around the cage, struggling to shake himself free.

An End and a Beginning

Cherokee inched his way along White Fang's throat, slowly throttling him. Just then, a dog sled and two men drew up the creek. It was clear that White Fang would lose and was close to death. Beauty Smith, furious, began kicking him savagely. The shocked new arrivals rushed over, and one of them punched Beauty Smith hard in the face.

"You beast!" cried one of the newcomers. "Cowards!"

White Fang lay bleeding on the floor, half dead.

"Matt," one man said, "how much is this dog worth?"

"I'd say $300, Mr. Scott," he replied. "Half in this state."

Weedon Scott thrust $150 at Beauty Smith.

"I ain't selling," said Beauty Smith.

"Yes, you are, beast. Or I'll hit you again."

For two weeks, Weedon Scott and Matt nursed White Fang back to health. When Matt unchained White Fang, he threw him meat, but another dog rushed in to take it. Like lightning, White Fang attacked the dog. Matt rushed in with a club, and White Fang bit his leg. Scott tried to calm White Fang, lowering a hand to pat him. White Fang leaped, biting through his hand.

The next day, Scott tried again. He offered White Fang meat. White Fang snarled, but he ate the meat thrown to him and, eventually, even took meat from Scott's hand. He shrank in terror as Scott reached to pat and rub his head. But the feeling was surprisingly pleasant.

It was the start of a new life for White Fang—one in which he knew kindness for the first time. Slowly, Scott undid the harm done to White Fang by humankind. White Fang's liking for Scott turned to love—the first time White Fang had felt love. He grew to like being petted. He still growled, but with a low note of affection now for Scott, his new god. He learned to tolerate Scott's dogs and accept Matt. He would greet Scott silently, showing his adoration with a steady gaze.

But one evening, Scott did not return. Day after day, White Fang waited. The wolf stopped eating and became sick. Matt wrote to his master:

"That wolf won't work. Won't eat. He misses you. Might die."

White Fang lay by the stove in Matt's cabin. One night he whined, and went to the door. The next moment, Scott came through it. White Fang snuggled his muzzle against Scott's body. The men were astonished. Within days, White Fang was better and leading the sled team.

A while later, as Matt and Scott prepared for bed, they heard a commotion.

"The wolf's got somebody!" Matt said. Outside, a man lay in the snow, covering his throat. They hauled the furious White Fang off him and dragged the man to his feet. It was Beauty Smith. On the snow lay a chain and a club. Matt turned him around and sent him off into the forest. White Fang growled.

The Trail

White Fang knew something terrible was going to happen. He whined outside the door of the cabin and stuck close by his man-god.

"That wolf's onto you," Matt said.

"But what would I do with a wolf in California?" Scott said. "He'd kill all the other dogs. He'd cost a fortune in lawsuits. He couldn't cope with the heat."

Then one day, White Fang saw Scott's bag on the floor and Scott packing things into it. That night, he howled. The next day, he followed Scott everywhere. The bag was joined by more, and an Indian took them to the harbor.

"Give me a last, good-bye growl," Scott said, rubbing White Fang's ear. But he wouldn't. They locked the cabin doors with White Fang inside and went down to the harbor, where the steamship *Aurora* waited. White Fang howled his utter misery.

Matt helped Scott with his bags and shook his hand as the ship prepared to sail. But then his hand went limp as he stared past Scott. White Fang was sitting on the deck. He came to Scott. There were fresh cuts on his muzzle.

"He came through the window!" Matt said.

"I'll write to tell you how he does," Scott said.

"You mean you're taking him? You'll have to clip his fur in the heat."

The ship sailed and Scott bent over White Fang.

"*Now*, growl!" he said, rubbing him affectionately.

When the steamer docked, White Fang was appalled by the bustle and noise of San Francisco. Soon he was locked in the baggage car of a train. When it stopped, they emerged into clear countryside and streaming sunlight.

A man and woman approached, and the woman put her arms around Weedon Scott's neck. White Fang became a raging, snarling demon.

"It's all right, Mother," Scott said. "He thought you were going to hurt me. He'll learn."

White Fang had a lot to learn. They went by carriage to a large house with sweeping lawns. No sooner was White Fang out of the carriage than an angry sheepdog set upon him. She was a female, and it was against his nature to attack her. He could only block her assault with his shoulder, and follow the carriage. Suddenly, a huge deer-hound leaped at him. He was running so fast White Fang was knocked over, but was quickly up and snarling. The sheepdog, Collie, saved the deer-hound's life, coming between them. Scott arrived, grabbing White Fang as Judge Scott, Weedon's father, called off the dogs.

That White Fang alone was allowed inside the house marked him as special in the eyes of the other dogs. Only Collie continued to bully him, knowing he would not fight back. White Fang learned he could hunt on their land, Sierra Vista, and wild land, but not neighboring fenced lands. He could kill wild animals, but not dogs. He followed his instincts until scolded.

He tolerated but never befriended other dogs. That urge had been driven out of him early on. He grew happy and softer, but never showed affection. He let the family pet him, but would romp only with his master. Weedon's wife, Alice, was wary of him around the children.

He often ran beside Scott's horse as he rode. One day, the horse threw Scott off, injuring him. Scott sent White Fang home. Reluctant to leave, at last he sped to Sierra Vista and growled, pushing the family around and alarming them. Eventually, as he tugged at Alice's dress, Scott's sister said:

"I do believe he's trying to speak!" For the first time, White Fang barked.

"Something has happened to Weedon," Alice said, understanding at last. White Fang earned an even warmer place in the family's heart after that.

A while later, Collie was uncharacteristically friendly toward him. They chased and frisked, and White Fang was driven by instinct to go off with her.

Soon after, the newspapers carried the story of a violent criminal, Jim Hall, who had escaped from prison. He had been treated unfairly, and eventually he had killed a guard and escaped. A reward in gold was offered, and packs of men with dogs tried to find him.

Some were carried back dead or hurt. Then Hall disappeared, the trail cold. At Sierra Vista, the women were scared by the reports.

It was Judge Scott who had doomed Hall to fifty years of hell in prison. Hall had been set up, but Judge Scott didn't know that. To Hall, Judge Scott was the enemy.

One night, White Fang became aware of someone inside the house, someone who should not be there. He crept silently to the foot of the stairs. As the man lifted a foot to go up, White Fang leaped onto his back. The noise of biting and tumbling and gunshots woke the household. Weedon and Judge Scott found a man lying still and White Fang near death, half-crushed and shot. They turned the man over. It was Jim Hall, dead.

The best doctor was called for White Fang, but gave no hope for his survival. For weeks, the girls of the house nursed White Fang. He slept for long hours, whimpering and snarling through bad dreams. But at last the bandages were removed. There was a party to celebrate, and Weedon's wife called him "Blessed Wolf," a name that they all adopted for him.

"He'll need to learn to walk again," the doctor said. "Take him outside."

They walked slowly toward the stable. There, White Fang found Collie with six puppies. She gave a growl, but one of the women picked her up. First, one puppy flopped in front of White Fang and licked his nose. Then, to Collie's disgust, the others tumbled over him. After only slight reluctance, White Fang lay in the sun, eyes half-closed, with his puppies gently mauling him.

About the Author

Jack London was born in San Francisco in 1876. His family came from a working class background, and as a teenager Jack took on many different jobs, from selling newspapers to shoveling coal at a power station. He also enjoyed adventures and managed to travel as a sailor—experiences which helped inspire his writing. Jack found fame and success with his novel *The Call of the Wild* (1903), which was set in the Klondike Gold Rush, as was *White Fang* (1906). He wrote more than 20 novels, and many short stories and essays. He died at the age of 40, at his California ranch.

Other titles in the *Illustrated Classics* series:
The Adventures of King Arthur and His Knights • *The Adventures of Tom Sawyer* • *Alice's Adventures in Wonderland* • *Anne of Green Gables* • *Black Beauty* • *Greek Myths* • *Gulliver's Travels* • *Heidi* • *Little Women* • *Peter Pan* • *Pinocchio* • *Robin Hood* • *Robinson Crusoe* • *The Secret Garden* • *Sherlock Holmes* • *The Swiss Family Robinson* • *The Three Musketeers* • *Treasure Island* • *The Wizard of Oz* • *20,000 Leagues Under the Sea*

An Imprint of Sterling Publishing
387 Park Avenue South
New York, NY 10016

Text © 2014 by QEB Publishing, Inc.
Illustrations © 2014 by QEB Publishing, Inc.

This 2014 edition published by Sandy Creek.

ISBN 978-1-4351-5827-6

Editor: Carly Madden • Editorial Director: Victoria Garrard • Art Director: Laura Roberts-Jensen
Designer: Martin Taylor

Manufactured in Guangdong, China
Lot #:
10 9 8 7 6 5 4 3 2 1
11/14